A Short Story

The *Fourth* Son

Terry G. Dodd

Copyright 2020 by Terry Dodd

The Fourth Son
Published by Yawn's Publishing
2555 Marietta Hwy, Suite 103
Canton, GA 30114
www.yawnsbooks.com

All rights reserved. No part of this book may be reproduced or transmitted in any form, electronic or mechanical, including photocopying, recording, or data storage systems without the express written permission of the publisher, except for brief quotations in reviews and articles.

The information in this book has been taken from various sources and is presented with no guarantee of its accuracy. All photographs used were submitted for this publication. We assume no liability for the accuracy of the information presented or any photos used without permission.

Library of Congress Control Number: 2020919044

ISBN: 978-1-947773-93-6

Printed in the United States

CONTENTS

Preface, Dedication and Acknowledgments   1

PART 1: **IN BEGINNING**
Wyoming - Real Time Backyard Talk   5

PART 2: **FLASHBACK**
Iowa - 1935   11
Hitting the Road   16
Go East, Young Man   19
Confrontation   24
Boston Bound   29
New Start   32
Winds-A-Blowing   37
South or Bust   41
Farm Country   48
Life Lesson   57

PART 3: **RE-START**
Family   65
Times Intensify   68
Settling In   73

PART 4: **BACK AGAIN IN REAL TIME**
Revelation   79
Deep Data Mining   81
Burt and Gene   84
Unanswered Questions   90

About the Author   93

Terry Dodd

Preface, Dedication and Acknowledgments

This is a lengthy short story inspired by real people and actual events. Its writing has come about through a surprising and dramatic personal revelation, but this is not a documentary. Some scenes, characters, characters' names and backstories incorporating artistic imagination are written to support the underlying story.

I dedicate this work to the following: My half-brother, B. Donald Ackerman, who thirsted for knowledge of his heritage; to genetics genealogist Joann Dunham, who applied enthusiasm and professional expertise to an intriguing parentage puzzle; to the memory of Max Eugene Dodd, Don's and my biological father; and to Don's and my two departed younger brothers, Michael Dean Dodd and David Lane Dodd.

I thank Helga, my personal and incredible IT and encouragement resource who has ridden alongside me for the fifteen years of our blessed marriage. I also thank those who troubled themselves to read my manuscript and comment on it before I sent the whole thing off to my favorite publisher. Lastly, but certainly not least, I thank God for blessing, straightening and leading both my ways and my days.

Terry G. Dodd

Part 1

IN BEGINNING

Terry Dodd

WYOMING – REAL TIME BACKYARD TALK

It was mid-summer of 2020 and Ingrid called down to her husband from the second story balcony of a modest rental home just outside of the small town of Pinedale, Wyoming, a stunningly beautiful hour's drive south of Jackson Hole. He was pitching horseshoes in a backyard framed by the Wind River Mountain Range. The first time Gene had brought up the idea of a summer vacation in such a remote location, his wife was instantly game, but asked about his motivation. He thought for a moment before giving her the short answer: "Mountains refresh my awe of God."

"Honey," she said, "that upstate New York genealogist you've been communicating with is calling. Pick up on the porch extension." To that, the German born-and-raised wife added, "And stomp the dust off of your boots before you come in."

"What?" he said, frowning, as he looked up. "Tell her I'm out in the 'back forty' wrangling steers."

His pragmatic wife, who had retired nearly ten years earlier as a twenty-plus-year administrative assistant for several different CEOs with a large German company, replied, "Gene Dawson, she knows you're a Georgia-boy and that we're renting this place in order to beat a month's worth of Georgia's summer heat and killer humidity."

The *Fourth* Son

"*Iowa*-boy," he said with a sigh while dropping two horseshoes onto a steel bench. "Georgia is merely where you and I live, worked, raised our separate broods, and met and married, all in that order." *Now what?* he thought. *Genealogist Jean has likely tracked down a few more genetic markers having to do with some shirttail relation in Timbuktu matching up with her adopted client's natural interest in learning about his heritage. Oh, well.*

"Gene," the genealogist began, her tone of voice betraying excitement, "sit down. I have some news that may be shocking to you."

"Really?" he said, more focused on needing only one more ringer from two pitches to set a new personal record of twenty-five ringers in a 100-pitched horseshoes set.

She knew she didn't have his full attention, but she was certain that would change. After a number of previous conversations, they had gotten to know one another a bit. "Take a break from your chores, cowboy."

"Pitching horseshoes isn't a chore; it's therapy. What do you do for relaxation in New York, Jean-with-a- 'J'?"

"What relaxation? I still work for a living. Okay, let me tee it up for you. What do you think are the odds of two elderly men living nearly a thousand Appalachian Mountain miles apart discovering through DNA that they are half-brothers?"

With yet another frown on his face he said, "I have no idea, but as you know, half-siblings are pretty common in my family. My father had two half-brothers and two half-sisters, plus one stepsister and one stepbrother. Whew!" Not knowing exactly where she was going with the inquiry he nevertheless decided to play along. "But in my case, I would say the odds are about the same as my pitching ten ringers out of ten tries . . . dead zero."

Ingrid was still on the line and smiled to herself.

As for the genealogist, she knew that after a year-long search, her day and that of her client Burt had already been made, but now it was the other half-brother's turn.

Part 2

FLASHBACK

Terry Dodd

IOWA - 1935

Early one morning, George Dawson began his counseling effort anew. "Son, what are you going to do now that you've been fired from your second job after completing your one-year college education?"

"Hey," Mack began his weak line of defense, "I'm from the enterprising strain of Dawson's. Remember? I've had two gigs now as a trumpet sideman with touring big bands, and one was for a two-day weekend at the Val-Air Ball Room in Des Moines."

"And your next gig is where? Having won a trumpet contest in high school isn't going to get you a seat in the brass section with Lawrence Welk's Biggest Little Band in America."

"Yeah, dad, I know. Look, I got a lead out of yesterday's newspaper. I'm applying for the job before noon today. Here, take a look." He pulled the newspaper clipping from his pocket and read from it: "Young men between eighteen and twenty-two and free to travel.' That's me."

The father contorted his lips as he said, "What about your girl-friend, Mickey? You know the one you were going to elope with until her parents and we convinced you to wait until you get beyond being jobless and penniless?"

The boomerang question caused Mack to tighten his own lips before answering. He only vaguely realized that hormones and emotions had been fighting common sense. "Okay," he said, "so that was a dumb idea, but I'm about to solve the problem."

The *Fourth* Son

At mid-morning, Mack walked into the hotel's banquet room only to see about 60 other boys his age either sitting or standing around. He walked up to a reception table where a young man his age said matter-of-factly, "Print your name here and take a seat. The interviewer will speak to everyone in about ten minutes."

Mack sat down next to another applicant and said, "Excuse me. What's the deal here?"

The fellow looked up, shrugged, and replied, "I don't know. The scuttlebutt is selling magazine subscriptions. What do you think of that?"

"That depends. Two years ago I sold enough newspaper subscriptions to win myself a year's worth of college."

"Wow, now that's something! As for me, I was selling the bejesus out of shoes until I got fired."

"What happened?"

The young man laughed, saying, "I couldn't satisfy the old fart of a store owner about the *correct* way to put shoes back into their boxes. All *he* ever did was to sit in the doorway of the back room playing solitaire and watching me sell shoes." With that, he put out his hand. "Name is Walt. What's your story?"

"Mack! Good to meet you. I'm a farm boy. My dad and his two brothers raised sheep for years on a little farm they called a ranch. That is, until the depression of '29. I'm one of eight children out of one father and two mothers. My biological mother died when I was three years old. The plague took her. My dad couldn't handle it and farmed me and my two-year younger brother out with relatives while he took his grief west for a year or so."

Walt shook his head and grimaced. "That had to be tough."

"You bet. He told us years later, though, after he had gained his teaching certificate, that the Lord had shown him his *manifest*—dad's word—responsibility and motivation to move forward. He married again and our families were joined. Sorry, I hadn't meant to go on like that."

"No problem. I don't have many friends who would be as open to sharing as you."

"Okay, you guys," shouted a fellow in his late twenties as he strode purposefully to the front of the room. "Give me your ears. This company I've been working with for the last five years has the finest commission deal in the publishing business. All of our successful salesmen earn a whole lot more than farmers, teachers and clerks. We represent all the top magazines in the country, everything from *Life* magazine and *The Saturday Evening Post* to *Readers Digest* and *The Farmer's Almanac*. People not only need to read, they want to read. Magazines are a lot more interesting and entertaining than either radio or newspapers. But this is what you came to hear: Once a week you will be putting half of your subscription sales into your pocket."

He took a few moments to intently look around, directly engaging many of the eyes of those in the room. "Now we only have two slots open for our traveling crew headed east the day after tomorrow. Each one of you who think you can sell will pick up a kit when you leave in a few minutes. You have until five o' clock this afternoon to see how many cash subscriptions you can sell. Even today you will put half of that into your pocket. The two men with the most sales will win the two jobs."

The two newly met young men turned to each other and shook hands while saying, "Good luck!"

Walt shrugged and said, "You know something. Eighty percent of these guys won't sell a single subscription."

Mack took that as a challenge. "I won't be one of those. This job is mine."

At 5 P.M., both men were again sitting side by side in the hotel room. Walt said, "How many guys do you reckon are coming back with something to show for their trouble?"

Mack looked around, counted, and said, "Maybe fifteen. How many subscriptions did you sell?"

"Three, and I came pretty close to pushing another one into the shoebox; how about you?"

Mack laughed and said, "I don't have a problem putting shoes into a box. I got four."

The two of them got the jobs. With good-byes to family that evening and a mother's help in packing a suitcase full of clothes suitable to the job at hand, along with promises to separate coin-washed whites from colored ones, they were ready to launch themselves into adventure and opportunity.

Terry Dodd

The next morning they both piled themselves and their gear into the crew manager's car and drove off. Mack left his tearful girlfriend with the promise of returning in 6 months with enough money in his pocket for them to get married.

The *Fourth* Son

HITTING THE ROAD

Before they were an hour out of town Mack posed two questions for Al, the crew manager, who was driving and sitting next to Ed, the fellow who had manned the reception desk: "Where are we headed and what's the sales pitch?"

Al replied with enthusiasm not much tempered relative to his hotel presentation. "Tonight, men, we will be staying in Monmouth, Illinois. Once we get to our hotel, Ed and I will explain the sales story and the team procedure. Tomorrow morning you can practice with one another for a while and then we will hit the neighborhoods at about 11 A.M. Eat a hearty breakfast. You will be mostly traveling by shank's mare. Lunch will be the extra apple or orange you take with you from breakfast."

"Shank's mare?" questioned Walt.

The crew manager smiled into the car's rearview mirror. "We'll be using that part of the leg between the knee and the ankle. It's called walking."

After a modest dinner paid for by Al at a small nearby restaurant he role-played with Ed. Narrating his own presentation, he began by saying, "With enthusiasm and using your own last name, boys, say, 'Hello, ma'am, I'm one of Bill Brown's sons working my way through college by selling magazine subscriptions.' And by the way, guys, it helps to know the name of a local university just in case your prospect asks. In this case it would be Monmouth College."

He continued. "Say, 'These magazines have the kinds of stories and color photographs everyone loves to see and read about. Here's one of my favorites.'" The lecturer held up a *Saturday Evening Post* issue with one of Norman Rockwell's paintings on the cover. "Okay, you see the point about creating interest in the magazines. So then you go to the first close, something like this: 'The cost is minimal, much better than the cover prices. Won't you help me out by taking a year's subscription?'"

Next, he reinforced what he considered critical: "Now hear me, men. It's important to not vary the pitch. Why? Because it's proven to work! Unfortunately, I can't actually make demo calls with you because two strangers standing at someone's door means what, to most people?"

"High pressure," Walt correctly ventured.

"No," Mack wisecracked with a smile, "Jehovah's Witnesses."

Everyone laughed. Lots of questions followed, with the manager answering every one with a positive spin, often followed by a statement such as, "Many others no better qualified than either of you have had great success." By way of comparison in making that comment he pointed to both himself and Ed. In fact, Ed had been with the company for barely more than a month.

The first day working in the field was challenging for both Mack and Walt, resulting in zero sales. That evening, however, the manager critiqued and encouraged both their delivery and memory of the prescribed routine. The next three days saw each of the two rookies make their first two sales, thus gaining for them much enthusiasm about the opportunity to make serious money. As they headed to the next town or village, Mack and Walt, both sitting in the back seat of Al's year-old Packard sedan, shared with the other more of their personal history, thus serving to add to their initial bond.

Terry Dodd

GO EAST, YOUNG MAN

It was March, and from their first small town sales beginning to the next they continued traveling and working neighborhoods eastward through Illinois, Indiana and half of Ohio, each day driving half of it before the crew manager dropped off all three salesmen plus himself, at different, but close-by neighborhoods. En route to this day's destination they passed through Peoria, Illinois, a city pretty much located dead center within the lower forty-eight United States. Mack couldn't help but wisecrack about the political cliché, *How will it play in Peoria?*

Narrator's Comment: Of course Mack had no idea at the time that his son Gene would be born there to him and Mickey some three years hence.

The crew's dogmatic pitch continued to prove successful, although Mack more than once suggested to Al that the appeal of the magazines themselves might have stronger appeal than the sympathy hustle. That did not sit well with the crew manager and he was not bashful in saying so.

For each community neighborhood's session, the routine was for each of the three to continue knocking on one door after another until the appointed time and place for the manager pick-up of each salesman. Not often, but sometimes they worked a town two successive days. They always kept half of each two-day weekend for travel and the other half for something like seeing a movie, shooting pool or sometimes playing duckpins.

The *Fourth* Son

In a small town a few miles north of Columbus, Ohio, Mack knocked on a door answered by a bearded man in his fifties. When given the standard line about working to continue his college education, the prospect asked if Mack was attending college there in town. Mack, who, upon arrival in town had made a quick phone call to the local library to learn the name of the town's local college, adroitly dodged the question by replying, "Actually, I am thinking of transferring from Ohio Wesleyan to Ohio State."

The university professor surprised him by saying, "Well, that's where I teach. When you visit the campus, come by my office and I'll tell you about the Geology department."

Mack's reply to that was two-fold: the first was to move things away from that subject, "I'm really more interested in sales and marketing, but thank you." The second was to smoothly shift the subject to the value of his magazines and the knowledge of a fascinating upcoming *Life* magazine article and photographs taken of the Grand Canyon.

Later that day, Mack shared with Walt that particular experience and the resultant subscription order. "You know," he said, "I would bet that *Life* magazine must buy photographs and articles every year about the single biggest tourism draw in America."

Moments later he asked himself why he had said that to Walt. Knowing that his earlier statement about the upcoming article concerning the

Grand Canyon had no basis in fact, it may have been Mack's conscience covering the making of a factual statement without specific knowledge of its truth. At any rate, he blamed the verbal stretch on the job.

Within a month they had traveled as far East as Pennsylvania, successfully selling subscriptions. They worked through that state and then traveled North up and through Syracuse, New York to the much smaller town of Utica, about 30 miles east of there. During that last stretch of driving, Mack and Walt complained to Al—practically in concert—that they needed some time off. After some thought, the crew leader said, "Tell you what, boys. If the three of you book a combined total of six sales yet today, we'll all stay an extra day and do something interesting tomorrow. I could use a little downtime myself."

Mack was up for both the challenge and the potential reward and he doubled down. His enthusiasm showed results with two subscription sales before knocking on a door answered by a woman and her high school senior daughter named Jillian. He nodded deference to both of them and began the standard pitch about raising money to continue his college education. The mother interrupted, saying, "Do you live around here?"

To that question, he would typically reply with something vague such as, "Not too far away, ma'am." This time, however, he felt called to be more conversant than usual. He replied, "No, ma'am. I'm visiting from out of town, but I really like the area, especially this neighborhood. Just this morning I read that New York Mills was named for a textile mill in the early 1800s. Tomorrow, the three college friends I'm traveling with and I are talking about taking a break and either going for a little hike or maybe playing duckpins. Is there is a duckpin alley in town?"

The daughter found the young man's appearance, mid-western accent and poise interesting. She was a tennis athlete, a swimmer, and of an independent mind. She spoke up, saying with a wink, "So you have taken the time to learn the name of our suburb? Well, we don't have an alley here, but there is one in the vicinity, in Utica. I've only played once, but that is one fun game."

"Wow!" an enthusiastic Mack responded. "So, Jillian, would you mind being a tour guide for this visitor? I'll spring for lunch for the two of us while the guys take a hike." He laughed at his joke about dumping his pals before adding, "And if your mother decides to favor me with a magazine subscription, we'll be back in time so that I can write up the order and get it into the mail."

This time, it was the girl's turn to laugh. "Is that how they teach you to close?" Then, with a defiant look at her mother, she said, "I'm going to take Mack up on the offer, Mom. You do your part."

Before noon the next day a rousing game of duckpins had been played by the two, along with much talk and laughter. Afterward, they had lunch at an adjacent hamburger joint. When they returned to her home, Mack picked up the mother's subscription order and thanked both the mother and father for their hospitality, saying, "You know, in this farm boy-turned-magazine salesman's experience it is pretty rare for what we call a 'subscription family' to take an interest in an outsider. I was just about to tell Jillian here that our crew ought to be back this way in a month or so before we head south and west. I'll stop by and tell you about our visit to the sales tour's northern point in Maine."

"Do that," the mother said, patting him on the shoulder. Mack shook the father's hand, and they all said their goodbyes. At the door, the daughter gave him a little peck on the cheek. He blushed, smiled and went on his way.

The *Fourth* Son

CONFRONTATION

Vermont was both a pleasant and profitable run across the Green Mountains and up to a village resort just the other side of the New Hampshire border by the name of North Conway. Sales had been off for Mack the past two days. The following morning, he and Al got into it again. This time it had nothing to do with the sales pitch, but rather their route and the almost daily move from one town to the next in which to ply their trade. "Who worked out this route?" he began. "Why do we pass through more towns than we work?" It seemed to Mack that such decisions were random and counter productive.

"Well, I'll tell you the way it is," Al said in his best manager-to-rookie tone. "Given that I'm not only the crew manager but the guy who owns the car and pays for the gas, guess who makes the rules? As it turns out, I also have an important business appointment to keep in Maine. After that we can slow down a bit. Besides, you're doing okay."

Mack had been thinking about things and wasn't about to let that be the end of the subject. "You're right about one thing. Yes, I have done okay, at least until the past few days, but for every two dollars I earn I imagine you also earn one." Then he stepped out onto a slim limb.

Walt and Ed were both present at the moment, so Mack glanced at each of them as he rebutted Al's response. "Doesn't the manager have responsibility for crew morale?" he said. "I mean, why don't we stay twice as many days in one town, thus doubling our earnings over a two-day period while cutting our driving time in half?"

That stuck in Al's craw and he wasn't interested in shaking it off. "I told you I have an important business appointment to keep. Now, by your own admission you've been slacking off lately. You were the only one of the four of us who didn't book anything either yesterday or the day before. What have you been doing with your time, checking out pool halls?"

At that, Mack held himself in check just long enough to figure out the best response. "Tell you what, Al, let's you and I have a little contest. Whichever one of us books the most business the next three stops, including one day in Dover-Foxcroft, wins the other guy's earnings for the week."

Both Walt's and Ed's eyebrows arched dramatically before jumping into the fray. Walt pleaded, "Hey, that's no way to resolve differences! We're all on the same team, just trying to make money to take back home."

"Yeah, that's right," said Ed, who almost never had anything to offer in discussions.

"Button it up, Ed," Al said in dismissing him. "And as for you, Walt, I'll take you on as well as your sidekick."

"Sorry, I'm not a gambler. Come on now, be civil about this, guys. Tomorrow will be a better day."

The *Fourth* Son

Al glared at Mack, saying, "You're on, Mr. Dawson."

Mack feverishly worked his three assigned neighborhoods over the next three days, employing his theory of stressing the value of the magazines rather than their programmed fast-talking hustle. For example, when he held up a copy of *The Saturday Evening Post* with a cover featuring one of Norman Rockwell's paintings, he used words like, "This most popular artist of our time actually refers to this magazine as 'the greatest window in America,' the point being, Mrs. Customer, that his work reflects small town American life, just like it is in your town."

He set a record for himself of ten subscriptions in a three-day period but would not share that result with the others until it was time to settle up at the showdown in Dover-Foxcroft. Neither did any of the others do any sharing of sales successes.

That evening, when the four of them gathered for dinner, it was pouring down rain. With a beer sitting in front of each of them, Mack said, "What do you have, Al?"

The crew manager was his usual boisterous self. "Well, now, let's just calm down, boys. There's no rush. First of all, dinner's on me. You see," he bragged, "I outdid even myself in this little contest." With that, he spread out his subscription orders as if they were a poker hand and his four 'cowboys' had just been called. "The final toll comes to thirteen subscriptions. Read 'em and weep, Mack-my-boy!"

Mack was less surprised than suspicious and said, "Does your entire reunion family live in Dover-Foxcroft? You know what I think? This whole Maine finale has been a set-up."

At that, Al stood and all but shouted, "Lay down your cards! If you can't beat thirteen, you're not only done . . . you're fired!" At that final word there was the slightest frown on Al's forehead, likely realizing he had just cut himself out of a steady sales override on a good producer.

Mack also stood. As he did so he pulled ten orders out of one pocket and the cash payments out of another. His words were terse, "I only have one request." With that, he turned to look squarely into the face of the fourth member of the crew while saying, "Let's see *your* orders, Ed."

Ed's face suddenly turned red. "Look, I had a bad spell. I haven't felt well all week." As he finished his excuse, he fished out the single order and its cash, adding, "I couldn't come up with more than one subscription, and I got it today."

The next morning, as Mack and Walt were each finishing up a light load of laundry in their motel's laundry room while saying their goodbyes, Mack emotionally thanked his pal for his friendship. Walt shook his head in sadness as he said, "What are you going to do?"

"With Al having claimed all my commissions for the week I have only two dollars in my pocket. The

The *Fourth* Son

rain hasn't quit, but neither have I. I'm going to Boston and to what I hope is my future. God help you, my friend."

Terry Dodd

BOSTON BOUND

Mack said to himself as he stuck out his thumb in pointing down the road to the south, *my future may begin in Boston, but first I have to get there.* With a road map, courtesy of the small hotel's desk clerk/owner, he plotted his approximate 250-mile trip, subject to hitchhiking travel vagaries. The intent was to travel through Bangor, Waterville, Augusta, and Portland before heading into the home stretch for Boston, the headquarters of his former magazine sales company employer. He would be in no hurry, however, because he needed to work the small towns in between the larger ones in order to cover his meals and the cost for a couple of cheap hotel stays.

Employing the same subscription sales technique which had gained him the solid performance of the contest with Al, he arrived in Beantown with a short stack of orders and the cash validating them.

"How may I help you, young man?" said the company's receptionist.

"I would like to see the sales manager."

Noting that he was not particularly well dressed, she said with the warmth reserved for door-to-door encyclopedia salesmen, "Sales applicants need an appointment."

Ignoring her response he said, "Tell him his former salesman, Mack Dawson from Iowa, wants to see him."

The *Fourth* Son

She considered that to be an impertinent request and gave him a look as if to say he wasn't about to get past this gatekeeper without a greater degree of humility than that. But then she thought better of her job in the still-precarious recovery from depression times. "If you'll have a seat I'll see if the General Sales Manager is available."

She was surprised when the sales manager told her to send the fellow right in. Mack was surprised with the manager's opening words: "Well, so you are the young man Al fired. I was disappointed to hear that because I know you had been generating some excellent business. I'm told you think you have a better presentation idea than our proven pitch."

Before he could verbally respond, Mack's thoughts ran to *he took the words right out of my mouth.* Recovering, he said, "Yes, sir. People in general are still stunned by what they have had to endure through the stock market crash and its aftereffects. They crave something besides what the radio and newspapers have to offer. Your magazines are that very thing . . . but we should let those stories and photographs speak for themselves, rather than running a hustle."

The sales manager was taken aback, having been prepared to lecture, if not *turn* this obviously motivated rebel. "Sit down and tell me more, young Mr. Dawson, but first I have another question for you. How did you manage to get from Dover-Foxcroft to Boston?"

Terry Dodd

"Thank you, sir. Let me tackle that last question first. I hitchhiked. As for covering the cost of meals and three nights in cheap hotels, I sold subscriptions on the way." At that point he pulled out of his pockets a pack of orders and laid them on the manager's desk. "I also have here the Company's $130 for its share of the subscription payments. The other half stays in my pocket."

Narrator's comment: $130 in 1935 adjusted for inflation, is equivalent to nearly $2,500 in 2020.

The sales manager had gotten to the position he held due to his favorite cliché, belief in actions speaking more loudly than words. He rose from his chair and walked around to Mack with his hand held out to shake, while saying, "I can see now that Al came up a little short in the managerial department. How would you like to be rehired with a promotion to crew manager and a sales override?"

Mack's eyebrows rose and his body followed as he accepted the offer. As he left the office, he was told he would also be given advertising support to hire a crew. "And oh, by the way," the GM added, "I saw the salesperson's signatures on Al's orders for those three days. Eight were his but the other four of his claims were Ed's. Your ten sales won the personal bet. Your commissions will be repaid to you . . . along with *his*. Congratulations, young man."

The *Fourth* Son

NEW START

The company did as the general sales manager promised. They ran classified ads in several of the Boston newspapers and then backed up Mack in interviewing dozens for a three-man sales crew. Mack conducted the final interviews, which resulted in a tough decision to take on an eighteen-year old, but who had successful newspaper subscription sales experience. He also hired a dynamic pair of twenty-year old twins who had sold encyclopedias the summer before. The two were taking a year off before their senior year at university in order to avoid taking on new loans. Their names were Jim and John. In a quirky decision, Mack said to them, "I find it difficult to tell one of you from the other, so for the time being I am going to call both of you "Jay." They laughed but didn't complain.

Mack was naturally appreciative of the company's support, but he asked the GM for one more item. "I need a car," he said. "I can buy a relatively low mileage 1930 Model A Ford standard Tudor sedan today for $250. Give me a 6-month loan for it and take $40 a month out of my commissions until I'm square. Do that for me and fill it up with gas and I and my crew will be on the road day after tomorrow."

That all happened. He alerted his new crew to be ready to leave town for a four-month sales tour. Because Mack was a first-time visitor to the northeast he chose to take a historical start by heading to Plymouth, MA and Mystic, CT before heading a bit west and then south. As before, the crew targeted smaller communities between the larger ones. With training imparted to the rookies before leaving, they were able to hit the neighborhoods running.

A week later, they found themselves in the Scranton, PA area. It was there that the youngest and least productive member of the crew bailed, declaring that he missed both his mother and his girlfriend. Mack said to him, "We have been on the road for not much more than four days. How did you figure to stay out for four months?" He wasn't looking for an answer. He drove the young man to the bus station and paid for his passage back to Boston.

Later that same day he phoned the company GM to tell him that things had started well, as could be determined from the subscriptions he was sending in, but that one of his boys had fizzled out on him the day before. "Will you do me a favor, sir? Contact Walt Larimer, my co-worker on dear old Al's crew and tell him to meet me in Scranton in two days? I want him in my crew."

Walt showed up and it was a joyous reunion as the two got caught up on things. That's when Mack said, "We will be headed south within another week, but first we're going to back track to Utica."

Walt's eyebrows went up as he said, "Did you forget something there?"

The *Fourth* Son

"Yes, a promise. But I'll tell you what. First, let's all take a half day off to refresh ourselves. Then we'll work our way up to Oneonta, New York."

"Perfect!" Walt exclaimed. "Let's see if we can find a place to swim. I want to make a hole in the water." All four managed that before the day was out.

They then worked the town for two days before driving on up to Utica. Mack let Walt run the rest of the crew's work day while he phoned Jillian. She answered, and without at first identifying himself, he said, "Ma'am, would your father be interested in a magazine subscription to either *Popular Science* or *Mechanics Illustrated*?"

"No, I . . . wait . . . Mack?"

"Yes."

"What are you doing in town?"

"I knew I wouldn't be back this way again because I have my own crew now and we're going to work the southeastern states. It's a long story, but I'm doing well and probably won't get home to Iowa for another four months or so. I told you I would stop again and bring you up to date. A lot has happened. Can I buy you a soda?"

They met downtown and played duck pins for an hour or so before grabbing something to eat at the alley's adjacent hamburger stand. She picked up the conversation with, "I won a fall tennis tournament in town last week and got a little trophy. Of course it wasn't anything like winning the Better Times regional women's doubles contest with my partner, which I did the year before. I don't think I told you I got to go to Chicago as the result of that."

"Congratulations," he said enthusiastically. "I don't know anything about tennis. What I do know a lot about is being fired from a job." He then shared the saga of the sales contest in Dover-Foxcroft before being fired and then hitchhiking and selling his way to Boston. He modestly described the meeting with management and his promotion and that he also got a car out of the deal.

She was confused. "So, if you are headed south, why did you go to the trouble of backtracking?"

"Oh," he began, a little nervous, "you and your family treated me so well that I wanted to say thank you in person. I certainly miss my family back home, but for a short time yours was the closest thing to that." Then, with a little hesitation he added, "after all, I'm still trying to find my way forward in life."

She nodded, saying, "Me, too."

Like most 17-year-olds, she was confused about life. For example, she didn't know what she liked about school other than playing tennis. The athletes she knew in her senior class all seemed to have the grace of goats. This visitor from a state she had barely heard of was not only handsome, but gracious and interesting. "Why don't you have dinner with us tonight?" she said.

After dinner and a little table conversation Mack said something about going out for a milk shake. The mother exclaimed, "An hour after eating two slices of my home baked apple pie and you're hungry again?"

"Hey, I'm a growing boy. It's June and the night is young. I'll have Jillian back in a couple of hours."

It was midnight when he did, but he wouldn't accept her invitation to come into the house, only as far as onto the front porch. He seemed reticent to talk, but finally said, "Look, Jillian, I don't know how to say this any other way, but I am promised to another. On account of that I'm ashamed of myself and embarrassed for you. Please forgive me."

"*Forgive* you? Why?" she said with an emotional mix of both hurt and surprise. "Like I said when you first came to our house to sell my mother a magazine subscription, I am my own person, and I am responsible for my own actions. Have a good life, Mack." With that, she went into the house alone.

Terry Dodd

WINDS-A-BLOWING

The crew was off on the first leg of what Mack was calling their "southern retreat." It would first take them to the northern tip of West Virginia before an eastward crossing of the Appalachian Mountains and then way south in Virginia.

One day, after an intense two weeks of half-day visits in smaller villages, they pulled into a roadhouse just outside of Roanoke at a sign reading, "Stay in a Wilderness Cabin Tonight." During the previous fortnight they had had only two days off for relaxation. Walt brought up the fact by saying, "What's with the focus on work, work, and more work ever since we left Utica? The guys are complaining that they didn't sign up for a no-break charge to the rainbow's pot-of-gold."

Mack was staring dully at his buddy, but not actually focusing on him.

"Mack," Walt said, "are you in there?"

"What? Oh, yeah. Sorry. I've been distracted lately."

"No kidding. I am amazed that your sales haven't been impacted. You're tearing things up. Even the guys are motivated by your personal production. But at the end of the day your mind seems to be unpacking a heavy load."

"Really?" he answered. *Is my mood that transparent?* He recovered with a laugh before lobbing a verbal grenade of his own. "Well, my good man, are you adding 'psychologist' to your sometime title of 'salesman?'"

"Good one, farm boy! Now you're talking. What do you say we kill something and eat it?"

"Okay, tell the boys to sleep in tomorrow. Maybe you can take a short walk in the wilderness with them in the morning while I write up the week's orders for mailing to Boston."

Everyone had a good time talking over the diner meal at a bar down the road which advertised fresh fried catfish. On the way back to the cabin, Walt said, "It's just as well that we're slowing down some tomorrow. One of the men in the bar said a big blow is coming tonight."

Mack tossed and turned all night. Whether it was due to the wind or his state of mind, he didn't know. When he got up the next morning, Walt had already left the room. He could see through the window that some branches had been blown down, but figured the guys were getting a little exercise before breakfast.

Once he had finished shaving and seen to his paperwork, he absentmindedly opened the small nightstand drawer. Glancing at a book inside, he wasn't surprised to see that it was a Bible, even though he had never before retrieved one during their many nights' stays in small hotels and cabins. This one had been placed there by the Gideons organization. Mack had never personally read much from the Holy Bible, but from time to time his father was known to quote various verses.

He opened the Bible to its very first page. There in bold print were the words, *"Help in Time of Need."* Below that were a dozen subheads, the last of which read, "*Forgiveness.*" It was not lost on him that he had recently used a form of that very word. That thought seared his mind. Fortunately for him the verses being referred for the reader to look up (1 John 1:8-9) also had a page number with it.

He read the two verses to himself and then read them a second time, but this time he read them more intensely: "*If we say that we have no sin, we deceive ourselves, and the truth is not in us. He is faithful and just to forgive us our sins and to cleanse us from all unrighteousness.*" He let those words sink in for several moments, then fell onto the bed, his eyes wet for what had been bothering him for the past two weeks.

First of all, he knew he had been unfaithful to his engaged girlfriend back in Iowa. Secondly, he felt just as badly for Jillian even though she had been as willing as he. That triggered something she had mentioned in passing, but which had not registered with him until this very moment. *She said she and her parents attended a Presbyterian church. A church!* What might that have meant to Mack? After all, he did not have a personal relationship with Christ, that is, he had never come close to surrendering himself and placing his faith in Jesus. He was, however, acutely aware of the guilt which had been building in him since they left Utica.

He was about to close the book, but something caused him to linger through another verse or two and then actually finish the chapter. A full hour later he had thoughtfully read, even pondering some of all five chapters of the apostle Paul's letter known as 1st John. Many consider that book to be the broadest coverage of the gospel in the entire New Testament. He flopped back onto the bed a second time, and for the first time in his life asked God's forgiveness. A seed of faith had been planted in Mack Dawson. Watering and growth would take yet another ten years, until his wartime service in the South Pacific.

Terry Dodd

SOUTH OR BUST

When Walt returned with the twins, he said to Mack, "Your eyes seem a little brighter. You find relief?"

"You could say that. I did some reading and found help in a book."

Walt noticed the Bible sitting on the stand but didn't mention it. Instead, he nodded and said, "Where are we headed, Boss?"

"South to Asheville, North Carolina, my boy! But on the way we'll check out a little town by the name of Boone. I think Daniel might have passed that way at some point."

Merely for the sake of conversation, Walt opined, "just because a town has the name of Boone, what makes you think Daniel spent time there?"

Mack's eyes sparkled at the opportunity to one-up his friend. "Two reasons; one, why else would a southern town be named 'Boone'? Two, they call this thing I'm holding, a road map, helpful to travelers. That is," he concluded triumphantly while giving his pal a knowing glance, "providing they can read."

Both Walt and the twins, who had by then joined the other two, guffawed in unison.

They managed Boone and then a few more subscription sales day forays on their way south. As they were approaching the outskirts of Asheville, they topped a steep hill just as the engine sputtered and stopped, drained of fuel. One of the twins calm-

The *Fourth* Son

ly said, "Throw her into neutral and don't let her stop. We just crested a good-sized hill, and I can see civilization below. If you mind the brakes, I think we might be able to coast into town."

Things happened in exactly that fashion. Once they creeped into a gas station, they were quickly attended to by a young man anxious to wash their windshield while filling the tank with 19 cents-a-gallon gas. Moments later they learned they would need more than fuel. The spare tire they had been forced to change for a blown one several days earlier needed to be replaced, along with the blown tire itself. While they were at it, Mack had the garage change the oil and give their flivver a minor tune-up. Fortunately, that only required replacing a couple of frayed hoses.

The car's ability to handle the Smokey Mountains was successfully tested in getting to Knoxville, Tennessee. Along the way they worked four different hamlets. Business was good everywhere except at the last village. For the first time since having left Boston the entire crew blanked. Mack called it a coincidence; Walt cited bad luck. The twins, however, spotted opportunity and called it an omen, claiming a break in town was needed in order to recharge their batteries. The four voted unanimously to accept the latter assessment.

After a morning's break shooting pool, Mack said, "Boys, we're gonna be in the saddle for a pretty good spell between here and Atlanta. Load up on whatever snacks you think will get you through. Who wants to cover me in the driver's seat?"

All three took turns, leaving Mack with navigator duty for most of the stretch. Hours later, Walt roused himself and sleepily asked of the twin who was driving, "Where are we?"

With a broad grin, 'Jay' said, "We're coming into a town with a big sign that reads, 'Roswell, Spared by General Sherman on his Way to the Sea."

"Looks prosperous enough," Mack commented. "Let's find a place to hang our hats for a couple of days and get to work."

The next morning before breakfast, Mack said he had a message for everyone from the Company's GM. "Congratulations are in order," he began. "When I talked with the big boss early this morning, he said we set a company record for a single crew for a two month period. Each of us will be receiving a 15 percent bonus on all our business during this coming month. What do you think about that?"

Naturally, they were excited, but they also thanked Mack for his leadership. He added to their motivation for the coming month by saying, "What this really means is that now we have even more opportunity to make 'hay' towards our personal goals for whatever comes next in life."

Two events happened as the foursome continued southbound and eased into Tallahassee. Day one went well enough. The second day, however, was interrupted when a police car pulled up to Mack as he was exiting a home where he had

The *Fourth* Son

booked several subscription orders with an enthusiastic couple who said they had two teenagers who looked like those in one of Norman Rockwell's magazine cover paintings.

"Young man," one of the two policemen in the vehicle said to Mack through the car's rolled down window, "What are you guys selling?"

"Magazine subscriptions," he replied. Then, in what would be ill-advised sarcasm given the circumstances, he added, "That isn't against the law is it?"

"As a matter of fact, it is, wise guy. Let's round up the rest of your crew and visit the sheriff." Within thirty minutes the crew was standing inside the jailhouse while being told they were violating Green River ordinances.

"What's that?" Mack's brow furrowed as he asked.

The sheriff was more than happy to answer the question. "It prohibits individuals from engaging in door-to-door sales or solicitations unless the community residents have given their consent."

"Since when has that become a law," Walt asked.

That gave the eager-beaver authority even more license to share his knowledge. "Since 1931, so named after Green River, Wyoming first banned such solicitations."

Mack followed Walt's objection with an off-the-cuff statement that put them at further risk. "I'd be willing to bet that law is still under First Amendment appeal."

The sheriff weighed in once again. "Appeal or no, you boys are subject to a fine. I've called in the judge."

"Sheriff," Mack said in quickly deciding on a different tactic, "May I make a reverse charge phone call to our General Manager in Boston?"

"You can, if you have a dime."

He did. The GM took Mack's call and after Mack had apprised him of the situation he asked to speak to the sheriff. The sales executive—having been through all sorts of sales field flaps over many years—calmly called the officer by his title and said, "Look, sheriff, I'll bet you also know it is illegal for businesses in your town to attach anything to a resident's mail box or its post, including flyers. Now, if even one person should complain to the post office about a single instance of that happening, the business risks being fined."

The GM let that sink in for no more than five seconds before following it up. "I know our boys have seen evidence of that sort of activity in town and they surely don't want to register a complaint. What do you say we call this whole thing off and they will leave town first thing in the morning?" That took care of that.

The second event took place the next day as they pushed a few more miles south in the crew's deepest advance of their 'southern retreat.' After a successful session in a panhandle village with the odd name of Sopchoppy, they stopped at a general store on the way back north. While there, the twins picked up a brochure touting a newly opened Florida state park named Wakulla Springs, about fifteen miles from where they were. It offered an irresistible draw. Back in the car the twins took turns excitedly suggesting they make the Springs their night's stop. "After all," said one, "we need some recovery time after our run-in with the Law." All four laughed before Mack readily acceded to the threesome's clamor.

The park and its lodge were located without much difficulty. A sign in the lobby claimed the Springs to be the largest and deepest freshwater spring in the world. A curious Walt gently challenged the desk clerk, saying, "How deep?"

"You won't be getting to the bottom, son," said the wizened attendant, happy to be engaged in conversation. "It's 185 feet." Then, with a smile, he added, "But it's so clear you can see all the way to the 'gators resting on the bottom." When the attendant told them they could actually "swim with alligators and manatees," all four lost no time in checking in and then dashing down to the small, sandy beach and plunging into the year-around 70-degree water.

After the swim and some dinner in the lodge, Walt said to an unusually quiet Mack, "Have you ever seen anything like that? I mean I saw an alligator sunning on the opposite shore that must have been 12 feet in length."

"No. Never." he commented, obviously occupied with another thought. "But you know something, Walt, a combination of that police situation earlier today and the clarity of this incredible spring has caused me to realize I don't really have a clear sense of where I'm headed in life. What is my focus?"

"Focus?" The sidekick said as he turned up both of his palms. "You're selling magazine subscriptions in order to build up a little nest egg. The same as this Iowa boy!"

"Okay, but follow me on this: Let's say we make it home within a month or so. What then? I don't have any job prospects. I know I don't want to go back to college."

Walt shifted tactics for his best friend. "Look, don't let your 'dobber' get you down. I'll play 'shrink' for you. First, you'll take the dough you've been stashing in the proverbial 'sock' for months now and invest it in some sort of little business. You'll work it hard for a while, then marry Mick and start raising kids. After that, you'll find the next adventure, hoping it won't be war."

Mack raised his head, his eyes brightening as he said, "Now that's a plan I can see happening, Sigmund Freud. What do I owe you?"

The *Fourth* Son

FARM COUNTRY

Mack plotted the home stretch. It would see them traveling through Mobile, Alabama to Greenville, Mississippi and then to Pine Bluff, Arkansas and Jefferson City, Missouri before arriving back in Des Moines, Iowa, at which point he would be putting the twins Jim and John on a Greyhound bus back to Boston.

As he told Walt and the twins, however, yet remaining in front of them was a good four or five weeks of sales efforts which should serve to pad everyone's pocket. That night, he called home for the first time since having left Iowa. His father answered the phone. After answering the 'How is it going?' questions, Mack asked his father if he would check in with Mick for him and give her the update.

"Call her yourself, son," he said. "She and her mother just got a phone."

He did. She was excited to hear from him and to hear something of his adventures. It was sweet conversation, but he kept it short, saying, "This is long distance, you know. I'm trying to save money for us."

She didn't care. "You get home, Hon! I want to hear church bells ringing."

The crew worked their way as planned for the next three weeks, taking a little time off each weekend, but still giving the sales effort their full attention. Late one afternoon an idea popped into Mack's head. He had been trying to think of a way in which he could provide inspiration for getting everyone's battery recharged for a strong dash to the finish line. That night he made a very different phone call.

Early the next morning—a Sunday, meaning it was a travel day for the foursome—just as they were about to depart their last stop in Arkansas for Missouri, Mack said to the others, "Listen up guys! I have some good news. We're going to take a little time off before we get on to Jeff City. You will absolutely love this. It'll be a good drive today, but if this tin lizzie holds up, we'll make it by nightfall."

The three were instantly excited. "Where are we going," asked Walt.

"For now, you drive. I'll navigate."

Nearly 350 miles later, traveling on nothing much more than narrow, two-lane roads rolling through hills and valleys behind tractors and hay wagons, Mack turned onto a long gravel driveway leading up to a flagstone farmhouse. They were in a Lake of the Ozarks village named Camdenton. As they came to a stop, Mack said, "Welcome to my Uncle Bill's farm. He's the youngest of dad's two brothers, Bob and George. I made a call last night and gained us a gracious invitation to spend a few days with them. Aunt Dorothy is the best cook in the state of Missouri." Everyone excitedly piled out of the car.

At the same time, Bill and Dorothy and their two mid-teenaged sons and younger daughter—having heard the automobile's approach—all came out to welcome them. "We hope you haven't eaten yet," the cook said in a strong Marjorie Main-like

The *Fourth* Son

'Ma Kettle' voice. The Boston-born and raised twins were already eating up the farm environment. Even though it was nearly dark they wanted to see the working barn. The patriarch, however, squelched the request. "Not this evening. Tomorrow will offer plenty of time for that."

Everyone contributed to the dinner talk. Walt was curious about something the Uncle had said to Mack, so he pursued it. "What was that about you and your two brothers once having a sheep ranch in Iowa? I'm an Iowan myself, just not from a farm."

"Yes, as a matter of fact our place was near Winterset, just south of Des Moines.

Mack, here, was born a few miles away in Norwalk. Lots of Dawson's are buried in a cemetery near there and another one in nearby Truro. All of those villages are in Madison County. When we still lived there, we often had occasion to travel through many of its beautiful, covered bridges."

Narrator's comment: Yes, those bridges would, sixty years later, be the site of Clint Eastwood's 1995 acting role and production of "The Bridges of Madison County." In the story, those historic bridges would become the photographic focus of the hit American romantic film about Eastwood's and actress Meryl Streep's four-day love affair which forever changed both of the characters they played.

The uncle decided to add one other thing to his travelogue inspired by the visitors. "And that reminds me of something else you boys might find interesting. Mack, do you remember a neighbor boy in Winterset by the name of Marion Morrison? He was about nine years younger than you, but his family once bought a couple of sheep from us."

Mack had a blank look about that vague bit of trivia.

The uncle smiled and said, "Well I hear the young man is making a name for himself out in Hollywood, making Western movies. He changed his name. I think his folks said to 'John Wayne'."

Mack had neither any recollection of the boy nor familiarity with the name, saying, "I haven't seen many movies."

The twins, however, upon hearing the name, jumped in excitedly, saying, "Well, we have! He's a cowboy movie star."

In the next morning's pre-dawn, as Mack lay half-awake, he suddenly heard a strangely familiar, softly-creaking, yet lulling sound. It only took another moment for him to recognize what that sound had always meant for him as a youngster living on the farm. He was listening to the soundtrack for sheer country contentment, that of a big, nearby windmill whose blades were turning in a light breeze. Once again, his thoughts ran to the future and the prediction by Walt that he would find direction. To that comforting thought he added a qualifier: *Either I find direction, or it will find me.*

Before long, the other three of the crew were rustling about in their two guest bedrooms. At breakfast, with everyone present, the four young men began peppering the uncle about the day's possible agenda. Within an hour, the twins were joyfully riding on a tractor as Uncle Bill drove them around the property, inspecting everything from pastured sheep and cattle to the barn and the livestock pond. Mack and Walt preferred walking around the barnyard, taking in the country air and talking about nothing in particular.

A big lunch began with Aunt Dorothy whacking the head off of a chicken and plucking its feathers. Before long she would be deep-frying the hen and serving it with fresh vegetables. The foursome recovered by spreading out in the living room. Within five minutes, Uncle Bill walked into the room sporting a wry smile. He said, "Well, youngsters, are you taking your daily nap, or are you up for pitching some horseshoes?"

They all jumped up and ran outside while their recreational guide secured four horseshoes and proceeded to urge the boys to spade up the two pits. The twins, even though they had barely heard of the game, immediately challenged Mack and Walt to a game. Hefting one of the 2½ lb. horseshoes, the two Boston born and raised young men were surprised at the weight, and even more so in pitching one 40 feet to a one-inch diameter piece of steel. And as for a shoe's landing with its tines open at the stake, neither of them fared well. All four, however, were delighted with the activity.

That night, Uncle Bill fired up the big outdoor stone fireplace and cooked home-butchered beef steaks. Aunt Dorothy filled everyone's stomach with side dishes and homemade peach cobbler. The talk ran to a combination of some of the boys' magazine subscription sales experiences and Missouri farm life. Walt and the twins said that tomorrow they wanted to try their hand at milking. Mack laughed and said, "I've had all that I ever want. I think I'll go fishing."

The visitors had been at the farm for six days, with every day either exposing them to yet another interesting aspect of farm life or simply finding the air and farm environment invigorating. Anticipating their plan to leave in another day or two, Aunt Dorothy said with an impish smile, "Well, while you boys deservedly rest yourselves tomorrow, I think I'll treat myself to a little therapy."

Walt bit on her ploy, saying, "Therapy, Aunt Dorothy? What do you mean by that?"

"Well," she said, "by washing all of your dirty clothes, and maybe even introducing a few of your shirts to something I doubt they have ever met on this trip—an iron!"

Mack laughed the hardest of the four and said, "She really drew you guys into that one. But seriously, aren't we all glad to be able to help our incredible hostess with some therapy?"

Now it was Aunt Dorothy's turn to laugh.

As that Saturday afternoon drifted into evening, the grand outdoor fireplace area once again came alive with everyone enjoying the conversation as much as the food. Toward the end of the evening, Dorothy turned a routine 'good night' announcement into something altogether different. "Well, it's time for the kids and I to turn in. You men stay up as long as you like. After all, we have to be up rea-

The *Fourth* Son

sonably early in the morning. Church service starts at 10:30."

That stopped the conversation. The twins responded first with disclaimers. Jim said, "Uh, Aunt Dorothy" (as all of them had taken to calling her), "excuse me, but we aren't church folk."

With what almost seemed like a sense of pride, John added, "That's right, ma'am. In fact, we have never once attended a church service."

The matriarch, being at times more prickly cactus than sunflower, said with a smile, "Lordy, Lordy, boys. But don't worry, you'll do fine. Besides, it's time you were properly introduced to Him. Good night, all." With that, she collected the children and vanished.

The moment she left the room Walter weighed in, turning to the only one to whom he could complain. "Uncle Bill, we have had a great time here and we are indebted to you for your hospitality, but I have had my debut with church and found it lacking. No disrespect intended." The other three thought that would surely end the discussion.

Uncle Bill glanced at Mack, who didn't immediately say anything. Uncomfortable with both the silence and the circumstance, the nephew twice shifted himself in his chair before speaking. "Well, I know I could personally use some churching, but I agree with the others that we might be a little out of our element. I think I, too, will pass on the invitation." No one, however, stood as if to leave the room.

Uncle Bill slowly looked around the conversation circle, in turn engaging the eyes of each of the other four. "It seems to me, boys, that each of you somehow feels the need to do life your way rather than the Almighty's way. When I was a young man your ages, I, too, felt immortal and answerable to no one. But then life began to happen all around me, including my two brothers. Oldest brother George lost his young wife when Mack, here, was only three years old. Middle brother Bob's marriage soured and split, and then all three of us lost our ranch."

He let those things sink in for a moment before continuing. "Along the way, I came to realize that there is only one thing in life that has no potential for hurt, disappointment or failure. I am referring to the unconquerable One—the One who not only created everything and everyone, but also offers us spiritual immortality."

The four-man crew squirmed, almost in unison. The three looked to Mack to provide for them a way out. Taking his cue, he made a half-hearted effort, "Tell you what, Uncle Bill . . ." he began, but then hesitated when his uncle gestured to him with a wave of his hand.

Uncle Bill had the floor and took it. "I understand, men. I know what you're saying. You're convinced that there is no guarantee you will come out of a visit to church tomorrow that will have made it worthwhile. Well, I am going to make you an offer. When you attend church with us tomorrow I guarantee you will come back here for lunch believing

The *Fourth* Son

that you will one day look back on the experience as much more than merely having attended a small church service in a small town in Missouri."

The boys knew there was no way they could get out of this. Mack summed it up for all of them, saying, "Man, oh man, could we have used you more than a few times on the road when we needed a professional closer." That brought forth nodding, grim-faced "Yes sirs!" from Walt and the twins.

The Uncle, however, had not made his guarantee without some inside information. Aside from knowing that the gospel message itself would be shared, as it always was, he knew the pastor had invited someone special to deliver the message that Sunday. One of the small church's biggest contributors was a first cousin to Dr. Harry Ironside, the evangelical pastor who had been preaching at Moody Church in Chicago for the previous six years and had already become well known across the country. The member had offered his cousin a free week's vacation at his cottage on the Lake of the Ozarks if he would preach one Sunday in his church. That Sunday would be this Sunday.

Terry Dodd

LIFE LESSON

"Good morning, church," the local pastor began. "We welcome Bill and Dorothy Dawson's four young men visiting with them on their farm for a few days." With a glance in their direction, followed by one at another visitor, he continued. "As I mentioned last week, today we have a very special speaker. The Honorable Henry Allen Ironside—better known simply as 'Harry'—will be preaching today, and you will be blessed. We also thank his cousin, Abner, for inviting Harry to speak to us during his free vacation stay at Abner's cabin on the lake." That remark brought muted laughter.

"First, let me share a few things with you about our speaker. Harry is a Canadian-American teacher, preacher, theologian, and author. At birth, Harry was thought to be dead, and so the attending nurses focused their attention on his mother, who was dangerously ill. Forty minutes later, however, a pulse was detected, and he was resuscitated."

The pastor waited a full measure before continuing. "No, he was not resurrected. That will not happen until Christ's second coming, assuming that doesn't happen while Harry is still with us." This time there was no muting of the laughter. "With that said, the pastor finished his introduction, "Please make welcome Dr. Harry Ironside."

"Thank you, folks," the guest speaker began, "for inviting me to visit your charming community, beautiful lake, and of course this fine evangelical church. First of all, allow me to say something about the title of 'Doctor', with which your pastor has titled me. I did graduate the eighth grade, but I certainly do not recommend my literary route. At age thirteen, I rested on the Word of God and confessed Christ as my Savior. At age sixteen, I began preaching full-time with the Salvation Army, some calling me the 'boy preacher.' Now fast forward to a time five years ago when Wheaton College presented me with an honorary Doctorate of Letters degree.

"Okay, folks, now allow me get to preaching . . . else there will be no honorarium for Ironside." With that, everyone laughed. "Seriously, folks," he continued, "there is a poem written in 1893 by English poet Francis Thompson, and it haunts me to this day. The poem is titled 'The Hound of Heaven.' If you aren't familiar with this famous 182-line poem, the short of it is this: 'As the Hound follows the hare, never ceasing in its running, ever drawing nearer in the chase, with unhurrying and unperturbed pace, so does God follow the fleeing soul by His Divine grace.' Isn't that beautiful? That line always reminds me of my own on-again, off-again Christian struggle between the ages of eleven and eighteen."

The preacher went on to share more of his life's challenges during that period and the decades to follow, making the point that all but One struggles with life and its problems to one extent or another. "Yet," he continued, "how important it is to recognize that there is that One who is unsubdued, undefeated and unconquerable, and that He is accessible to everyone who is willing to acknowledge Him."

After about 30 minutes at the pulpit, he glanced at his watch and said, "Let me make the following point and I will be through. The incredibly good news is that in Christ who loved us and gave Himself for us, we are *more* than conquerors! You say, 'Harry, what does that mean?' Well, ours is not a stoic resolve against mindless evil. Ours is a hope-infused courageous resolve because, come what may, the end will be glorious beyond all comparison."

He took another minute to briefly illustrate how everyone is vulnerable in so many ways, particularly so if they deceive themselves about not needing to be dependent upon Christ, the conqueror of one's soul. "So," he said in conclusion, "as the Hound of Heaven pursues you in never ending pursuit, allow yourselves the grace to be caught, and turn to Him. Thank you for having me here today."

Back at the farm, as Aunt Dorothy was preparing lunch for family, the four boys, and Harry Ironside, plus the pastor, his wife and his cousin and his wife, Mack took Uncle Bill aside to say, "I apologize for my and the other guys' rude response to your invitation last evening. We all have much to learn. As for this sinner, I hope the Hound of Heaven does not grow weary in its pursuit of me."

Ironside overheard the remark and took a step closer to Mack in making some encouraging observations. "Well said, son. Confession is the first step

The *Fourth* Son

of repentance. Make it a habit to meet with God—that is, studying His Word and being in prayer—and I guarantee the Hound will find you."

After the bountiful lunch had concluded and all the men were momentarily seated in the living room, the irrepressible Dorothy entered carrying a glass of milk. She went up to Mack and said in her inimitable fashion, "I noticed you didn't sing this morning. Was your throat dry or were you praying?"

Caught off guard, but not offended, he gently returned fire, saying, "Oh, no, it's just that people get really emotional when I sing." The room erupted into laughter. Harry Ironside laughed the loudest while slapping a thigh.

Late that evening, after everyone but family and the four visitors had left, Mack spoke to their two hosts. "On behalf of the twins, my pal Walt, and me, let me say that at first light we need to be headed to Jeff City, and then on to Iowa. But please know that this time with the Camdenton Dawson's has been the visit of a lifetime. Aside from the fact that a person never knows when he might have the opportunity to again cover ground with favorite people, such milestone visits as this one are very special. Thank you, thank you, and thank you."

Walt couldn't let his friend's philosophical comments go by the wayside without what he considered to be a "me too" remark. "Well, now, doggoned if this boy hasn't finally added the first touch of wisdom to his advancing years." That provoked one last laugh before the nighttime bed. Goodbye hugs would wait until early morning.

From that day and on until they drove into Des Moines a week later to load the twins onto a Greyhound bound for Boston, they plied their sales trade like the professionals all of them had become. Mack assured the other three that he would see to all bonuses being promptly and fully paid, along with any commissions due them. To lend assurance to that comment he added that he would call the GM that very day in asking for expedited clearance. Final and sincere handshakes and back clasps ensued.

Mack made his call to Boston and then drove Walt to his family's home in West Des Moines. On the way, Walt asked if the GM had had anything else to say. "Well, my friend, you recall my having told you I advised him several weeks ago that both of us would be packing it in once we got to Iowa. He said he very much wanted us to stay on, but I told him you and I had talked about it, both deciding we had run our course and needed to settle down and/or move on. He understood and said he would be sending each of us a letter of commendation and referral."

Walt responded with, "Good job, my friend. Oh, but I forgot to remind you about asking him to send you the title to your car."

Mack smiled and said, "No problem. I meant to ask myself, but he beat me to the punch, thanking

The *Fourth* Son

me for having paid off the car loan ahead of schedule."

Walt nodded and said, "Well, farm-boy. I don't want to tear up on you, but I am going to miss you. I think I'm going back to school to see if I can get a degree in something."

In a choked voice as they shook hands and hugged, Mack said, "Let's stay in touch." Sadly, they did not. He drove the few miles back down to Winterset to see his family and then set his car in motion for the 100-mile drive to Ottumwa and his future.

Part 3

RE-START

Terry Dodd

FAMILY

Mick didn't know which of two days Mack would be arriving, so she had paid even more attention to her dressing the second day when he had not arrived on the first. The greeting was overwhelming for both of them. It was September and she would not turn eighteen until May, while Mack would turn twenty in January. They would not marry until September two years hence, so until then Mack had to actively attend to career plans. That would not be easy. When he received the bonus money due him from the Company, he was blessed to count the amount in his 'poke.' That came to almost $500. In spite of that reserve, however, he had no job and no leads, thus the wedding postponement.

Narrator's comment: Again, with regard to adjustment for inflation, $500 in 1935 is equivalent in 2020 to nearly $9,500.

He wisely decided to put the money into a bank for the time being, but what to do in the meantime? After much thought and inquiry he decided to go back to what he had been doing some months before having embarked on the magazine subscription tour; selling advertising specialties. Unfortunately, but to no surprise, he found himself distracted by preferring to be in Ottumwa where Mick lived, rather than in his Des Moines territory, so he was once again fired.

In succession, he then tried selling tires, followed by the much more diverse work as a bookkeeper. Not really caring for either of those, he

The *Fourth* Son

took a job with a peanut vending company, shelling peanuts. That was boring work, but he kept his focus. Before long, he was promoted to route salesman, servicing and installing peanut machines.

Shortly after that his employer offered him a raise if he would move to their Peoria, Illinois operation. Welcoming that news, he and Mick decided to get married. Gene would be born in Peoria, but after about two years into the job Mack got sick and they moved back to Ottumwa, which is where their second son was born.

One day, not long after that move, Mack said to Mick, "You know, I really liked the freedom I had when I was my own boss. I'm going to go into business for myself." He took the money he had banked from his 20-plus state road saga and made two business decisions: First, he bought 75 peanut machines and placed and began servicing them. That didn't take all of his time, however, so he also became an independent contractor with the same advertising specialty outfit his father was then working for as sales manager.

Again, things went well for a few years until sometime in 1941. WWII! Business went south for both of his business endeavors. The family moved to Des Moines where there was more work. Mack and Mick both took jobs at an ordinance plant which manufactured military ammunition for the war effort; he as a security guard and she on the assembly line. It would be another few years yet before their third son would be born.

Then Mack caught a break. His family had always had horses on their farm, and he got wind of the company bringing in horses for security use. He applied for and was assigned to the firm's mounted patrol with a handsome gelding named King. In short order it became apparent to others that Mack was good with horses. His supervisor said, "You know, there's some extra money in it if you are willing to saddle-break some of these broomtails." Was he ever!

The *Fourth* Son

TIMES INTENSIFY

Fast forward yet again, this time to 1943. All four of Mack's brothers are on active duty; two in the Army, one in the Navy, and one in the Air Corps. Mack said to his wife, "I know you don't want to hear this, but I have to do my part in this war. We have a little money put away now and I need to enlist."

From time to time they had had discussions about his enlisting, She, however, always had a strong argument. "How am I going to raise two young boys on my own?"

1944 rolled around and the issue again came up. This time, however, given that their baby was thriving, she relented. "The boys and I will move in with mom so that you can enlist, but on one condition." Thinking there was somehow less risk in one branch of service versus another, she said, "You have to go into the Navy."

In June of 1944, Mack went down to the military recruiting office. "I'm here to enlist in the Navy," he said.

After some formalities, the Sergeant in charge said to the new volunteer, "You and the other enlistees line up over there." Once that happened, the sergeant said, "I need three volunteers for the Marines." Pointing, he said, "You, you, and you." The third "you" was Mack.

He was twenty-nine years old at the time and stated his objection, "But Sergeant, I'm married and have three children."

Terry Dodd

The Marine Sergeant responded with a smile, saying, "That's what I like in a Marine . . . maturity!"

That was it; he was a part of the 3rd Marine Division and headed for boot camp in San Diego, California. Shortly after his arrival, however, he heard about auditions being held for the 3rd Marine Division Band and their being one opening for a trumpet player. He wrote to Mick and asked her to ship him his trumpet.

He was obviously out of practice, but he had not only played well in high school and through his only year in college, but as earlier mentioned, he had even played some gigs as a sideman for a number of Big Bands touring Iowa.

Taking the trouble to learn a few critical aspects of the auditioning process, he elected to spend the allotted week's practice time solely on the same tune (*Flight of the Bumblebee*) which had won him his college scholarship. When that tune's turn came up for audition play, he literally blew the director away, winning a position in the 3rd Marine Division Band.

Shortly after that he shipped out for the South Pacific Island of Guam. En route from here to there on board the transport ship, which happened to be a converted liner and thus had a piano, he heard someone playing music. He approached the man with a question. "What's the name of that tune?"

The *Fourth* Son

The piano player responded with, "I don't know. It's an original composition and I haven't been satisfied with the words I've written to the music."

They began conversing and Mack said, "Let me give it a try." Within a day or so a new amateur musical team was born; a lyricist and trumpet player on the one hand, and a piano player-composer and saxophonist on the other. By the time the ship arrived on Guam, the chorus to "I'll Be With You" had been written. It was a piece which would not take long before becoming featured by the division dance band, Mack would also play in both the division's march and concert bands. The two would go on to write two more tunes together while they were in service together, all of which expressed the love-haunted loneliness of men away from their wives and sweethearts.

One day, word got out that Mack's 3rd Marine Division would be taking part in the Battle of Guam. That battle lasted for 21 days, after which came mop-up fighting and then participation in an Iwo Jima operation. After that, the Division was back on Guam preparing for the invasion of Japan. Fortunately, that operation never occurred because Japan surrendered in August of 1945.

Ironically, two events during Mack's time in the South Pacific would be more personally meaningful than the war itself. In the fall of 1945, he was notified that his seven-year old son had accidently suffered third degree burns on ten percent of his body by a leaf fire on the family's lawn. Gene would undergo multiple surgeries with skin grafts to his lower right leg from four other parts of his body. Mick was instrumental in initially saving the boy's life by following doctor's orders to sterilize a pair of scissors and cut the burned skin from the leg while waiting for the ambulance to arrive. She was up to the grisly task.

In anticipation of thousands of active duty servicemen shortly being released, the military sent Mack home on emergency leave and he was honorably discharged in November, 1945. That was a month or so before the 3rd Marine Division itself was deactivated. In the process of one of Gene's early surgeries, however, the surgeon advised the father that they would have to cut the leader vein under the knee in order for the leg to straighten out as it healed. Mack asked one question: "Will he walk without crutches?"

The answer was in the negative. "Then, don't cut it," he said.

The surgeon explained the consequence of Mack's decision: "In that case, Mr. Dawson, you will have to stretch his leg for him every day. He will scream and his grafted skin will bleed. Are you up for that?"

"I am!" was the reply. This time it was the father's turn, saving the child from a crippled life. It took more than six months, but the boy fully recovered with no limp and only a scarred leg to which he would quickly learn to point to as a badge of pride.

The *Fourth* Son

The second of the two events mentioned above was quite different. It happened before the other and a short time prior to the Battle of Guam, Mack had been in deep thought about that upcoming event, and after one particularly restless night he rapped on the door flap of the tent of one of the Marine Division's naval personnel. He had talked with the man a number of times about his relationship with the Almighty. "Chaplain," he began, "ten years ago I first heard about the Hound of Heaven. Well, he has apparently been pursuing me ever since. I am now desperate to have the LORD come into my heart and to be baptized in His name."

The next day, he wrote to his wife about his decision and the action he had taken. The Chaplain also wrote Mick a letter in which he explained that Mack had decided he wanted to come home to her and the boys "an active Christian."

Terry Dodd

SETTLING IN

Back home in Ottumwa, it wasn't long before Mack felt the need to move the family once again. This time, to central Iowa (Newton) where he would begin what would become a successful 40-year career in sales and top management in the same industry which in an earlier time had twice fired him for dalliance. What accounted for the difference?

He would ascribe the answer to that question in a 1953 cover story printed in *Salesman's Opportunity* magazine. The answer was three-fold: maturity, hard work and perseverance. As an aside, that same article also detailed Mack's multi-state magazine subscription sales odyssey at age nineteen through more than twenty eastern states, including New York state.

In what form did Mack find relaxation from work in his career climb? Among a host of interests, chief among them were golf, card-playing, and pitching horseshoes. But there was one hobby more special than even those: dancing with Mick. She was the more talented of the two, but together the couple would come to enjoy teaching ballroom dancing for such diverse groups as high school prom friends of the boys and close adult friends.

Not everything was roses, of course. Only a few years after the war the family took a summer vacation to a northern Minnesota lake with the two older boys, while the youngest, Lane, stayed at home with the maternal grandmother. Dean, the younger

The *Fourth* Son

of the two boys on the trip was fiddling around on the huge, rounded, rock cliff on which their rented lake cabin was situated. A light rain had just finished and the surface was slippery. Venturing too close to the cliff's edge, the boy slipped and tumbled more than twenty feet off the sheer edge into the lake. Hearing the screams of others, Mack ran down to the cliff's edge. Without hesitation he dove into the lake, rescuing his seven-year old son.

For the next year or so, he and Mick would make a joke of wondering about their *youngest* son and when the hat trick of their children's brushes with death would take place. Fortunately, that did not happen.

In 1975, something happened that would eventually prove fatal. Mack and his wife and two other couples plus their son Gene and his wife were on a golfing trip to a remote resort in Valles, Mexico, some 350 miles south of Brownsville, Texas.

Mack developed a serious stomach ailment, but in not speaking adequate Spanish and not knowing whether or not their health insurance would cover out-of-country treatment, or even if such was safe, he was reluctant to consult a local medical doctor.

The Mexican golf professional, who had played with Mack many times during past trips, had an idea. "If your son wouldn't mind going out into the jungle in search of a specific, but common tree, and cutting off an eight or nine-inch piece of healthy branch and bringing it to the resort kitchen, I will show him how to brew a tea which has excellent medicinal benefits for stomach ailments."

Gene accepted the challenge. He located such a tree as the golf pro described, cut off a length and brought it to the kitchen. Following directions given him by the golf pro he peeled the bark off of the piece and steeped it in hot water for the prescribed period of time. Draining the tea, he cooled the mixture and then gave it to his father to drink. Within twenty-four hours Mack was feeling some better, but after one more day and considerable deliberation he said to Gene, "Number One Son, will you drive me to the hospital in Brownsville?" Mack and Mick had driven down from Iowa, while Gene and Carol had flown from Wisconsin. Gene subsequently drove the four of them the seven-hour trip from Valles, Mexico to a hospital in Brownsville. The ensuing operation required a blood transfusion.

Narrator's comment: On special occasions Mack sometimes used 'Number One Son' in speaking to Gene. The term itself was coined for a popular 1940s fictional Chinese-American detective who traveled the world investigating mysteries. By including the use of 'Number One Son' in this story, Gene is using literature to transfer the honor from himself to Burt.

In the mid-seventies, donated blood was not always tested. As a result, tainted blood was introduced into Mack's vascular system. It would be many more good years before he was diagnosed with Hepatitis C. Fifteen years from the time of the blood transfusion to a prolonged and painful illness which included several surgeries, an otherwise

The *Fourth* Son

healthy Mack would succumb to the disease and prematurely pass at age seventy-four.

Part 4

BACK AGAIN IN REAL TIME

Terry Dodd

REVELATION

Gene was once again on the phone with the genealogist, but this time the call had been at his initiation. "Jean with a 'J', he said, "show-and-tell me how you arrived at solving your client Burt's mysterious puzzle as to 'Who dun it?'"

"I appreciate your interest in the details," she said. "Allow me to email you something about the process. Then you can ask me about specifics. In the meantime, however, I will give you Burt's phone number."

"Perfect," he replied. Hanging up the land line he turned to Ingrid and said, using the only complete German sentence she told him he would ever need, *"Das ist sehr gut, meine Frau."*

How did the first communication go between the two half-brothers? Burt answered Gene's call, and the conversation began something like this: "Burt, your genealogist family friend seems pretty certain that you and I are half-brothers. What do you think about that?"

No wallflower, Burt responded by saying, "I'm good. It is also my understanding that I am the *big* brother, and as such there is probably a pecking order here, *little* brother."

Gene's first thoughts were, *Wow, in all my 82 years I have always been the eldest son. Circumstances can change things.* After the call, the two got busy exchanging emails and enlightening each other as to biographies, immediate family, medical health, and even hobbies, which included mutual reading and writing interests.

Early on, however, it seemed that while their relative technology skills seemed to be comparable, they had both been left behind. It would also become apparent that there were differences with respect to other areas. One example would be politics—Burt being of the liberal persuasion and Gene of the conservative—but the more important element was that of family connection.

Many questions were prompted during their first Zoom meeting, hosted by genetics genealogist Jean. The two wives—Burt's Alice and Gene's Ingrid—were initially present for introductory purposes. For a full hour the two men responded to one another's questions, having to do with family, home situations and even varied personal interests. Given the country's coronavirus situation they would likely never develop a close relationship, but the critical connection was the revelation of their half-brotherhood.

Terry Dodd

DEEP DATA MINING

Jean responded to Gene's email request with information that shed interesting light on her search for a DNA match with Burt. She had begun the process by building an ancestry tree, creating what looked like a 'pedigree' view; that is, a timeline built from various source documents of supporting information for a particular person. Such documents included Census Records, Birth, Marriage and Death Records or Indexes, War Records, News Articles, Draft Registration Cards, Obituaries, Find-A-Grave, and of course relevant information gleaned from living persons who had had DNA testing.

She noted that each person had a gallery of images (photos or stories), which others in the world had that matched an ancestor of both Burt and all those whose information placed them foremost on the parentage prospect list.

Ancestry, however, was not the only database she used for pulling in records. Among the charts she sent Gene were copies of the first three pages of Burt's DNA matches with one of the primary ancestry databases. Another interesting attachment she provided was a fascinating DNA tool cleverly called WATO, standing for "What Are The Odds?" That chart showed Gene's paternal family ancestry four generations removed.

The research question Jean was asking of the database was this: Who was Burt's Father? Of those names which had markers (called 'centimorgans') of more than 600 cMs were of a Dawson cousin (Woody, 653), of a nephew (Patrick, 925), and of course, Gene himself (1,800)! Gene's big number was in the very highest match range possible. This meant that he would have to be one of the following relative to Burt: a grandfather, a grandson, an uncle, a nephew or a half-brother. Age ruled out everything but the half-brother.

What were some of the additional elements involved in our genetic genealogy detective's chase? Well, first of all, Jean followed the same methodology developed by the top genetic genealogists in the country, including the industry's most respected guru, who for the past five-plus years had been assisting law enforcement using DNA and genealogy methodologies to help solve crime-related cases.

Ideally, the paper trail should include having some evidence that places the two individuals in the same place, at the same time. Jean's comment about that: "But whether or not we have corroborating evidence, the undeniable DNA fact remains." The story-within-a-story presented in the earlier portion of this narrative, and which blends facts with fiction, addresses the key issue of opportunity.

Jean also had all of her data reviewed by two other genetic genealogists who supported her hypothesis. As a disclaimer, a DNA version of the popular cliché, "the proof is in the pudding," looks at all the supporting evidence, including any evidence that would help disprove a theory or hypothesis. In other words, the answer to Jean's question, "Who is the subject's father?" lies in the deep data mining of math, percentages and DNA recombination.

Mack's and Burt's shared DNA turned out to be *twice* that of any of the other closest markers, clear evidence that the two shared one parent! In other words, when the DNA thread of those numbers were compared . . . Bingo!

The *Fourth* Son

BURT AND GENE

As earlier noted, Burt was adopted when he was three years old from an orphanage in Utica. He has no memory whatsoever of the orphanage or of any time preceding that, including the adoption process itself. In growing up in a loving adopted home he served as an acolyte in the local Episcopal church, was active in Boy Scouts, and—as he describes himself—was a mediocre athlete in a small K-12 central school. He would also be well-provided for by his adopted parents.

Interestingly, Burt's post high school years somewhat matched Gene's in that both attended two different colleges or universities before graduation. Burt began his teaching career with 3 years as a fifth-grade teacher before spending the next 27 years teaching sixth, seventh and eighth grade social studies.

Oddly enough, Gene's strong university science focus led him instead to a career in advertising sales, management and entrepreneurship. As for their individual special interests, Burt leaned into local government and liberal politics ("my 'sport' is politics") while Gene combined writing with his deeply held faith convictions and conservative political leanings.

Again, more importantly than their divergent special interests are the things they hold in common. In looking at a few items on the lighter side, it is learned that both men were long-time rabid fans of the Brooklyn Dodgers baseball team. That is, until the team packed up and moved to Los Angeles. At that point both brothers promptly threw 'dem' Dodgers under the bus.

In addition, not only did both of the brothers serve enlisted terms in the U.S. Army, but each did so *before* marrying. Credit the maturity that often came to young men in their era through a dose of military discipline.

And speaking of marriage and having certain characteristics in common, there is the matter of unswerving personal commitment to spouse. Burt, *the older*, met his future wife, Alice, in college and they married after their junior year. They have been married for sixty years, raising two children: a girl and a boy

Gene, *the younger*, having met his first love in high school, married Carol before college. They achieved a successful forty-five-year marriage until her untimely death in 2005. Was it coincidence that before her passing she prayed with her hospice nurse that Gene would marry again?

How did that marriage happen? He and Ingrid met and married while both were serving in their church's Stephen Ministry program. That union is now nearly fifteen years young. As an aside, add those two marriages together, although such does not serve any purpose other than statistics, and he, too, could count sixty total years of committed Christian marriage. He has been blessed with three children (a girl and two boys) by his first wife and with one stepchild (an adult female) through his second marriage.

The *Fourth* Son

Allow me to back up to a time of challenge for each of the two half-brothers before managing to win a future wife. Burt had met Alice in one of their college classes and they took an immediate liking to each other. He could not help but notice, however, that she was wearing an engagement ring at the time. She explained that she was engaged to a boy from her hometown who was then serving in the U.S. Army.

As Burt tells it, "She didn't seem too devoted to him so I told her to give the engagement ring back to the boy's mother and we would get to know each other. She did and we did." Now that is style!

Consider the similarity to Gene's challenge after his third date with his future wife and mother of their three children. He had just begun his senior year in high school, and she had graduated a year earlier. She fairly shared with him that at the time she had three suitors, not counting the late comer. One of them had been in her high school class, the second from the class a year earlier, and the third was currently a naval cadet. Furthermore, she had been invited by the cadet to attend the upcoming Army-Navy game in Annapolis, Maryland.

To shorten the story, Gene mounted an outrageous courtship which caused her to gently dismiss the first two and cancel the football invitation with the latter.

So, when it comes to marriage, what did Jesus say to the Pharisees when questioned about the subject? He said to them, *Haven't you read the Scriptures? They record that from the beginning, 'God made them male and female.'* And he further said, *This explains why a man leaves his father and mother and is joined to his wife, and the two are united into one. Since they are no longer two but one, let no one split apart what God has joined together."* (Matthew 19:5-6). One pastor has intuitively stated that marriage is meant to mimic and reflect the relationship between Jesus and the church.

It is worth spending another few paragraphs about current interests of these two men. Burt is in the process of writing several quite interesting historical political works; one is a profile of George Lunn and the New York politics of his time.

As Burt writes it, the Reverend Dr. George Lunn was to become "a unique and potent force in Schenectady and indeed in the state of New York State politics." Schenectady is Burt's longtime area of residence. He goes on to explain in writing that around 1910 Lunn was the Minister of the First Dutch Reformed Church, one of Schenectady's most prestigious houses of worship. Burt goes on to tell us that the man used his pastoral positions to rail against the political corruption that was so rampant in the city and the nation.

Predating Lunn, Burt writes some fascinating material about the Dutch West India Company's Schenectady colony's history and its 1624 founding. The storied Mohawk Valley and the driving force behind what would become the community of Schenectady was a man by the name of Arent van Curler, born in the Netherlands. One of the challenges to his effort had to do with securing title to the land from the Mohawk Indians. How challenging was that? he asks. It was as if today a group of investors were able to buy a parcel of land from the Canadian government and have the United States government accept it as an integral part of the United States!

Lastly on this subject, one of Burt's most interesting introductory chapter comments is about the Dutch Reformed Church taking on what we today would consider governmental functions. The church, which was formed sometime around 1670, acted in many capacities, such as helping the poor and the destitute, loaning money, serving as a bank and a general store, and even taking in the homeless. Burt sums up the church as an institution that at the time was "the glue that held the community together."

As for Gene's special interest late in life, after having served successively for seven years in each of two different ministries—one as a volunteer board member with a hospital auxiliary, and another as a counselor with his church's primary evangelical affiliation in trucking food and the message of the gospel all over north Georgia—he turned to another very different way of serving.

Having read about Congress passing a law in the summer of 2019 that opened up American Legion membership to anyone having served any active duty military time, he signed up. He shortly accepted the local Post's offer to take on his retiring mentor's position as Public Affairs Officer. But the first thing to catch Gene's attention in that position was the opportunity to spur resurrection of the Post's mascot, a 105 mm Italian made howitzer captured in Iraq during Desert Storm.

With help from others he re-established the Post's newsletter and coined the name "Howie" for the howitzer. Needing both equipment and painting upgrades for both the cannon and its trailer, he secured donations to effect Howie's re-birth as a fundraising tool to aid the Post's American Legion mantra—"serving other veterans, the community and nation."

The *Fourth* Son

UNANSWERED QUESTIONS

Weeks after the initial half-brother revelation as shared by genealogist Jean, the younger of the two brothers began asking himself some questions tangential to the search. Jean had shared that she and Burt had figured out his biological mother's name. They also determined that she had gotten married close to the time she gave him up for adoption, but not why. And yet, all of that shed no brighter light as to who was Burt's father. But of course DNA has given us the answer to that question.

A different question bothering Gene was why his mother had apparently not saved his father's letters from his year-plus time overseas? That question led to even more: Were there ever *any* letters? The only letter found in the mother's effects after her passing was the one from the Guam Naval Chaplain to her about Mack's decision for Christ and his subsequent baptism.

Granted, although neither Mack nor Mick were known to be especially sentimental, that was especially so of Mick. Gene recalls that his mother had more than once said, "Even though we never told you boys we loved you, doesn't mean we don't love you."

Perhaps Mick *did* save some letters, but because of her guarded sentimentality she may have simply chosen not to pass on such personal letters to her sons. Or, had Mack possibly shared with her, in writing, something she simply preferred not to acknowledge to their children? Of course, all of this is sheer speculation.

And to this speculative exercise we could also add the question of whether Mack ever harbored conscious thoughts about the possibility of a true "fourth" son. Why the presumed term here of "son"? Only so because of the complimentary and honorary term both Mack and Mick used on occasion relative to their closeness to Gene's deceased best friend of sixty years, i.e., "Jack, we regard you as our *fourth* son." Why do we even ask such a question as this? Does not everyone have moments from the past which occasionally well-up in unintended recollection?

The final two unanswered—if historically inconsequential and absolutely speculative questions—are these: Did either Mack or Jillian ever inquire after the other, and if so, did either have anything to say of a relevant nature?

Last sentences of this story: Genetic genealogists tell us that autosomal (an adjective referring to inherited genes belonging to a person) DNA testing going as far back as six generations is very useful in determining genetic matches. There is, however, an important caveat: DNA testing is not all fun and games.

What does that mean? There are ethical considerations to such testing. DNA testing reveals family secrets! TV's crime-solving genetic genealogist CeCe Moore's favorite caveat is this one: "Someone's eye can be shot out." What does she mean by that?

The *Fourth* Son

Some people might not be happy with what is learned. On the other hand, it can also lead to forgiveness and healing.

The narrator of this story prefers the positive perspective, having invited Burt and Alice to visit and stay a few days with he and Ingrid at a time of the New Yorkers' choosing.

One last observation is that because Mack often referred to the wives of each of the three of his known sons as "daughter." The point is that if circumstances had allowed, Gene believes Mack would also have referred to both Burt's Alice and Gene's Ingrid as "daughter."

Finally, why are any of us created and for what purpose? It is easy to think our purpose in life is for whatever is best for us as individuals, but the fact is, as one pastor recently reminded his congregation, we are created for God's glory; for He is the kingdom, and the power, and the glory, for ever and ever.

—End—

Terry Dodd

About the Author

When I wrote my first book (*Uncommon Influence*) in 1994, I spent more money bringing it to print than all the other twelve books which followed, combined. That was before the days of self-publishing. Production costs for editing, formatting and typesetting came to $10,000. In addition to that, in order to keep the print run costs to a minimum I gambled by ordering 3,000 copies at three dollars per unit. Then there was another $1,000 charge for standard ten percent print overruns (300 copies) and shipping from Colorado. To answer my wife's marginally feigned cries of 'family irresponsibility' for the $20,000 I was obliged to siphon from our savings, I could only point to the fifteen pallets of unsold books sitting in my basement.

In seeking to deflect some of the home fire flak, I told her I had an idea to defray part of the *investment*. "And what is that hon?" my wife asked with raised eyebrows. "Well, dear," I stuttered, "I plan to sell advertising space in the back of the book at $1,000 a page." I did not, however, share my own producer's protests, incessantly insisting that, "No one will buy a novel with ads in it!" To my wife's delight, my producer's indifference, and my surprise, I sold eight pages!

I even managed to get the advertisers' cash up front, except for one who insisted on providing me with half of his fee with his own line of promotional products—plastic book marks, tip charts, playing

The *Fourth* Son

cards, and calendar card-mirrors with easels, all custom imprinted with the book title and my name.

My lovely wife had one further question: "Dear, now exactly how are you going to fulfill your promise to the advertisers to place 3,000 books into the hands of distributors in your southeastern states territory?" I loved that woman, but she could be such a nag.

I responded with one word: "Steadily!" It took me five years, but I personally sold 1,000 books at $14.95 each, delivering them in-person on distributor sales calls. Having dispensed with the middleman, I also managed to accomplish both my obligation and my promotional goal through a combination of 1) literally giving away 2,000 copies at national and regional trade shows and to the membership of several trade organizations, and 2) being coerced into accepting a free monthly 1/8 page ad as in-kind payment for a monthly column I industriously wrote for five years for the promotional products industry's premier trade journal.

Now, why, you may ask, have I reprised that decades-old, self-serving saga at the end of this odyssey about Mack, Burt and Gene? To make two points: Firstly, the problem with self-publishing is that without a significant marketing budget (of which I never had the benefit), one's book sales are guaranteed to be minimal. Secondly, even though the *UI* book's secular science fiction/mystery plot drew rave reviews it did nothing to advance the

Kingdom's needle, i.e., it made no attempt to shine the light of Christ on the darkness of this world.

So, here is the lesson I have learned about writing: If you feel called to write, you *must* write, if only for yourself; and if you believe the LORD has called you to write about Him, you had better be about that and the things of eternity. After all, God's Word is His plan for our redemption. As a result of such thinking, each of my succeeding titles have been evangelical in nature; some being Christian novels and some inspirational narratives.

And oh, yes, twenty years after *Uncommon Influence's* secular writing I wrote a Christian revision retitled as *Mirror Magic.*

The *Fourth* Son

Books by Terry G. Dodd

Some of these titles are out of print, but some are still available from Amazon, Yawn's Publishing, or even from me (dodd@bellsouth.net), with the exception of three revisions of earlier titles within the last-listed Gam'man Trilogy.

Self-Produced Title:
 Uncommon Influence

Self-Published Titles
 Fired with Enthusiasm
 Life's Toughest Lessons
 The Foursome
 The Carpenter
 Ancestors
 Hungry for Hope
 Journey with Outstretched Hands
 *Mirror Magic (*1st Revision of *UI)*
 Ultimate Encounter
 Unto the Heavens
 What a Wonderful Life

Gam'man Trilogy Revisions (Unpublished)
 Hidden Persuasion (2nd revision of *UI*)
 *Celestial Mystery (*Revision of *UE*)
 A Calling from Afar (Revision of *UH*)

For more individual book information, visit my website: terrygdoddbooks.com